I0669734

Essex Institute

The Fifth Half Century of the Arrival of John Winthrop

Essex Institute

The Fifth Half Century of the Arrival of John Winthrop

ISBN/EAN: 9783337293574

Printed in Europe, USA, Canada, Australia, Japan

Cover: Foto ©Andreas Hilbeck / pixelio.de

More available books at **www.hansebooks.com**

THE

FIFTH HALF CENTURY

OF THE

ARRIVAL OF JOHN WINTHROP

AT

SALEM, MASSACHUSETTS.

———

COMMEMORATIVE EXERCISES

BY THE

ESSEX INSTITUTE,

JUNE 22, 1880.

(From the HISTORICAL COLLECTIONS OF THE ESSEX INSTITUTE.)

SALEM:
PRINTED FOR THE ESSEX INSTITUTE.
1880.

INTRODUCTION.

THE two hundred and fiftieth anniversary of the arrival
of John Winthrop, at Salem, with the charter and records
of the Massachusetts Bay Company, occurring on June 22,
1880, it was deemed meet and appropriate that the first
field meeting of the season should be held on that day,
at the Pavilion on Salem Neck, from which is obtained
an extensive view of the bay, and of the shore along
which the fleet sailed ere the anchors were dropped in
the waters of New England; and that the exercises
of the occasion, instead of a discussion on subjects of
general scientific and historical interest, should be devoted
to a recital of incidents connected with this important
event, or such other topics as the time and place might
suggest.

A description of the appearance of Salem harbor, at this early period in our history, may be gleaned from the following extracts from the diary of Rev. Francis Higginson, who, under date of "Fryday, June 26, 1629," writes : "The sea was abundantly stored with rockweed and yellow flowers like gillyflowers. By noon we were within 3 leagues of Capan, and as we sayled along the coast we saw every hill and dale, and every island full of gay woods and high trees. The nearer we came to the shoare the more flowers in abundance, sometymes scattered abroad, sometymes joyned in sheets 9 or 10 yards long, which we supposed to be brought from the low meadows by the tyde. Now what with fine woods and greene trees by land, and their yellow flowers paynting the sea, made us all desirous to see our new paradise of New England, whence we saw such forerunning signals of fertilitie afarre off." On Monday, June 29, 1629, he writes : "we passed the curious and difficult entrance into the large and spacious harbour of Naimkecke, and as we passed along it was wonderful to behould so many islands replenished with thicke wood and high trees and many fayre green pastures."[1]

Much valuable information on this subject may be obtained from Rev. Joseph B. Felt's Historical Sketch of the Forts on Salem Neck, read at a field meeting on Salem Neck, Thursday, Aug. 20, 1863, and printed in the fifth volume of the Historical Collections of the Institute.

The Pavilion is located at or near the land granted by the town of Salem, of six acres, to Rev. John Higginson in 1661. This land was conveyed by deed (Reg. Deeds,

---

[1] See Hutchinson's Collection of Papers, pages 41 and 44.

Essex, vol. iii, fol. 396), 25, 9, 1670, to Thomas Savage, who on August 6, 1675, transferred the same by deed of gift to his daughter Sarah and her husband, John Higginson, jr., with lands adjoining which he had purchased of other parties, in all about twenty-eight acres (Reg. Deeds, Essex, vol. iv, fol. 383).

A grandson of John Higginson, jr., the fourth John Higginson[2] in succession (and the four were living at the period from the birth of the youngest Jan. 10, 1697-8, to the death of the eldest in Dec. 9, 1708) conveyed, April 8, 1730, to Benj. Ives (see Reg. Deeds, Essex, vol. lv, fol. 92).

After the death of Benjamin Ives in 1752, the estate with additional purchases, including land obtained from the town by vote of the citizens, in exchange for Pignal's[3] or Roache's Point, on which is located the present almshouse, amounting to forty acres, etc., passed into the possession of his son John Ives, who conveyed the same to Richard Derby[4] May 16, 1758 (see Reg. Deeds, Essex, vol. cxliv, fol. 40).

After the death of Richard Derby this property was

---

[2] Rev. John Higginson, born at Claybrook, Aug. 6, 1616, came with his father to Salem in 1629, and in 1641 assisted Rev. Henry Whitfield (whose daughter Sarah he married) in the ministry at Guilford, Conn. He returned to Salem in 1659 and was ordained as pastor of the church, which his father had founded some thirty years before, and continued the respected minister until his death Dec. 9, 1708.

II John born at Guilford, 1646, a merchant, settled in Salem; Lieut. Col. of the regiment, a member of the Governor's council. etc., died March 23, 1719.

III John born Aug. 20, 1675, educated a merchant, lived in Salem, died April 26, 1718.

IV John born Jan. 10, 1697-8, graduated at Harvard College, 1717; sustained chief offices of the town, County Register, etc.; died July 15, 1744.

For a sketch of this family see Hist. Coll. Essex Inst., vol. V, p. 33.

[3] This name appears in deeds, but it should be " Picton " named for Thomas Picton to whom the land was originally granted. Sometimes spelled Pigden.

[4] For a sketch of the Derby Family, see Hist. Coll., Essex Inst., vol. III, pp. 154, 201, 283.

assigned to John Derby towards his portion of his father's estate, who conveyed the same by deed to Edward Allen, Dec. 13, 1793 (see Reg. Deeds, Essex, vol. clvii, fol. 73). After the death of Edward Allen, July 27, 1803, and of his wife Margaret, Aug. 13, 1808, this estate passed into the possession of his son Edward Allen, who sold the same to Josiah Orne Feb. 26, 1810 (see Reg. Deeds, Essex, vol., clxxxviii, fol. 177). Josiah Orne, April 6, 1816, conveyed the same to Jonathan Dustin of Danvers (see Reg. Deeds, Essex, ccx, fol. 86). Eliza Sutton, Hazen Ayer and Serena his wife, in her own right, all of Peabody, being heirs of the late Jonathan Dustin, conveyed the same to Daniel B. Gardner, jr., of Salem, Sept. 24, 1875 (Reg. Deeds, Essex, vol. dccccxli, fol. 233), who has since had the land surveyed, constructed streets and avenues, and sold many lots upon which have been built a large number of seaside residences.

The forenoon of the day was devoted to visiting the various places of interest in the neighborhood. The inspiration of the occasion was not wholly in the memories of the past, but bright sunlight, refreshing breezes, the lovely green of the shore and the deep blue of the bay, dotted with the white sails of many yachts, engaged in their annual regatta that morning, added much to the enjoyment of the large number who participated in the celebration. At 1 P. M. lunch was served in the spacious and handsome dining hall upon the second floor of the Pavilion ; at 2.30 o'clock the formal exercises were held in the hall below in the following order :

ADDRESS.

By ROBERT S. RANTOUL.

THE Present and the Future are measurably of our own making. No act of ours, be it ever so trivial, but has its ever-widening circle of remote results. Not so the Past. We find that ready to our hands. It spreads before us like the canvas of the limner, inviting study, stimulating aspiration, inspiring thought; but, like the canvas of the limner, it makes no answer to our fascinated gaze. It lies revealed, like some crystal rescued from the caverns of the earth, immutable and perfect, and we contemplate it as something wholly outside of and beyond ourselves,—as something of which we had no hand in the making, and for which we are in no way to be called on to account. Nothing that we may do can make it other than it is. Nothing which we have done,—nothing which we have omitted to do, has helped one jot to make or mar its everlasting mould. It looms up before us, forever fixed, like some awful form unfolded in a vision, remote, inexorable, silent, and at rest forever.

Yet there is a sense in which all this is otherwise. If our children ally us with the future, so do our ancestors ally us with the past. The ancient precept, "Honor thy father and thy mother," is still in force. We are what we are, in great measure, because of what they were. And we may not study their acts as the acts of beings without personality,—as occurrences which entrance the

(5)

mind but cannot move the heart. On closer knowledge, the soul warms towards the actors of the past. As we walk among them familiarly, they seem to return our ardor. They reward our devotion. They reflect our feeling. And at last dry fact becomes living reality,— naked bones put on a fleshly garment, and the scenes that have been of old seem to breathe and glow again with quickened and responsive life.

It has been thought fit to commemorate to-day, by becoming observances at this spot, the advent of John Winthrop upon the shores of Massachusetts Bay. It is good to pause, on a day so marked, so fateful, in our colonial annals, and give ourselves up for an hour to the reflections which crowd upon the mind. It is wise to call up to the fancy the picture of that auspicious scene, —to recite the perils of the voyage,—the hopes, the fears, the aspirations of those engaged in it,—the aspect of the country they approached, and the condition of the settlements which were to be their future home. Especially has it been thought becoming, in the descendants of these actors in the past, to devote a portion of the day, consecrated as it is to heroic memories, to an effort to disclose and emphasize, if we may, the true significance of the occurrence we recall,—to an endeavor to compute the value of the contribution made to the great sum-total of American nationality by the little band who touched our shores two centuries and a half ago.

On Saturday, June 12, 1630, a date corresponding with the close of the third week of the fairest month of our New England summer, the hamlet which stood where we now live was roused at early dawn by the unwonted sound of cannon in the offing. Early risers paused in their homely avocations, and stood listening at their cabin thresholds; and the startled red-man, crouching for wild-fowl behind these very ledges, forgot his aim and strained his unassisted vision seaward. Among the wooded islands of the outer harbor was descried, sharply defined against the background of the glowing East, a single craft of no mean tonnage, flaunting at peak the red cross of England, standing in by the North Channel between Baker's Island and the lesser Misery, and dropping anchor as the sun reddens the horizon. The Lyon, Capt. Pierce, is lying within the islands, and that "Palinurus of the Bay" is not slow to hail the new arrival, a skiff from whose side had boarded him at early dawn. There is hasty interchange of salutations. Master Allerton, he who gave his name to the outer headland of Nantasket in Boston Harbor, is on his way in a shallop from Plymouth to Pemaquid, now Bristol, near Casco Bay, and as he sails by, having taken the wings of the morning, he boards the new-comer, within an hour of sunrise. Another shallop bears down the harbor from Salem, — there were early risers in those days, in Salem, — and at last the welcome story reaches the little hamlet of the presence of the "Arbella," flagship and pioneer of the expected fleet, of three hundred and fifty tons burthen, manned by fifty-two seamen and mounting twenty-eight guns, after a tempestuous, seventy-six days' passage from the Isle of Wight, bearing John Winthrop and the Charter of the "Governour and Company of London's plantacion in the Massachusetts Bay in New England." Local self-government had struck its roots in Massachusetts soil. Those morning guns, still echoing along our breezy headlands, had announced the possibility, now assured by five half centuries of successful trial, of tranquillity with freedom ; of a democratic commonwealth without class privilege ; of an equitable land tenure without primogeniture ; of the

independence of church and state and of political stability
without hereditary office. The purpose for which God
had at last unveiled the western world was about to be
achieved and the destiny of America was determined.

It would be delightful, did the hour permit, to picture
what Winthrop found here, with the fidelity of graphic
art. The material is at hand. We know who were here,
for the settlers of Salem had only moved up from Stage
Point, between what are now known as Norman's Woe and
Gloucester Harbor, fours years before, when the fingers
of the two hands were enough for numbering the heads
of families among them, and, since then, they had been
successively reinforced by Endicott and by Higginson,
with only a chosen few of England's best. We know
where these worthies lived, for the restless zeal of our
antiquarian students has left no record unexplored, which
could correct the outline map of the early town. We
know what our fathers wore, what arms they carried,
with what tools they wrought; for all they had of tex-
tile fabric or mechanical design came from old England,
and invoices and bills of lading, detailing fashion and
make and quality and price, are extant yet. Finally, we
know well what manner of men they were,—what their
purposes in life,—what their impressions of the new
world, for they were neither idle triflers nor uncultured
boors, but set themselves at once about recording obser-
vations and transmitting intelligence to friends left behind.
Nothing is more delightful than the perusal of these co-
pious details. They unlock heart-secrets; they repro-
duce the age. And when, at "about two of the clock"
on this anniversary day, so the narrative proceeds, "Master Endecott," whom Master Peirce had returned to Salem
to fetch, boarded the Arbella, and with him his pastor
Skelton and one Capt. Levett his adjutant, perhaps, it

is not difficult to picture the scene which followed. "We
that were of the assistants," continues Winthrop in his
journal, "and some other gentlemen, and some of the
women, and our captain, returned with them to Nahum-
keek." It is not recorded how they came up the harbor,
but that they came in sloop-boats, then called shallops,
and in common use, is a fair presumption. Nor are we
told just where they stepped ashore, although tradition
and conjecture point strongly to the curious metamorphic
rock, near the old Bass River ferry and the present Bridge,
as the probable landing. Somewhere along that grassy
eight-foot lane which skirted the Planters' Marsh and
hugged the margin of the stream, and which led on to
the Governor's "fayre house" and the Arbor Lot Fort,
that notable company must have disembarked and taken
their stately way on foot, to enter upon the mission of
their lives. They were men who had turned their backs
upon much that was worth living for in England,—men
whose eminent connections, whose intelligence, whose
character and whose means, made possible the establishment of a state and the building of a capital town in
this untrod waste,—men who were pioneering the largest
and best appointed fleet ever yet put forth for a port in
America,—men who meant, peaceably if they could but
forcibly if they must, to make fast and strong the foot-
hold of the Saxon race on this continent, and to make
the discomfiture of Richelieu's ambition absolute and final.
There is a native dignity in these men, arbiters of a continent, as they walk in sober state along the sunny stream.
No pomp attends their way. The hundred or more of the
village, old and young, are at hand to greet them; but
with conflicting feelings. The winter had been hard and
the help of the new comers is welcome. But the powers
which Conant and his men had, not without jealousies and

regrets, made over to Endicott, two summers before, Endicott must in turn surrender to another. Hardly corn enough remained for a fortnight's supply, and yet the Arbella brought no succor. No joy-bells pealed, for as yet no monitory church-spire cleft the clouds. The oaks, which were to frame the venerable church structure preserved to us through the beneficent liberality and zeal of a former President of the Institute, were tossing their branches in the vernal air. No cheerful salvos from Darbie's Fort or the Arbor Lot echoed the Arbella's sunrise guns, for then powder was precious, like dust of gold, and gunners were "fishers and choppers and plowmen" also.

Notable indeed was the seaworn company which sat at meat that day in the new-built Endicott cottage, and looked out from under its peaked gables and through its diamond-leaded windows upon the Indian village in North Fields and the grassy slopes of what we call Orne's Point, and supped there, as Winthrop does not fail to tell us, with a smack of the lips quite pardonable in one just landed from seventy-six days on shipboard, "with a good venison pasty, and good beer." And thus the "fayre house" which Higginson, in 1629 found newly-built for Governor Endicott was the first habitation in the colony to open its hospitable doors to his successor.

Winthrop, the central figure of this group, was in his early prime, at forty-three. A man of rare grace of person and bearing, he was not more marked by those traits which make men engaging in their intercourse with others, than by those more robust attributes which fit us to determine, to withstand, and to prevail. The ladies, at least, will allow me that he was no ordinary person when they know that at the age of seventeen he was a husband, and had embarked upon his third matrimonial venture at the age of thirty. At eighteen he was a justice of the peace, and at twenty-one, father of three sons, one of whom was afterwards Governor of Connecticut, and another of whom was drowned, near the scene of Leslie's Retreat, on the day after his landing. He had been educated at Cambridge, the liberal University of England; had ceased, in June, 1629, to be an attorney of the Court of Wards,—indeed, he belonged to a family learned in the law from the time of the 8th Henry, as well as pillars of the reformed faith even in the bloody days of Mary; he had joined Matthew Cradock's company of adventurers in September, 1629, on condition that its patent and entire concerns should be transferred to America, and had been chosen Governor in October, with the greatest confidence and hope, as Cradock's successor.

I dare not trespass on your time, to attempt a characterization of this distinguished personage. Such an attempt, limited by the narrow necessities to which I am bound, would do injustice to his name. Nor is there need of tribute at my hands. A descendant of his, whom we hoped for the pleasure of seeing and hearing to-day, has dealt in his own graceful, delicate and exhaustive way, with this eminent magistrate and man; and while no family portrait could be more fit to inspire ancestral reverence and pride, nothing which my researches have brought to light would prompt me to modify, in a single line, the noble features thus delineated, nor to question the exalted estimate put upon the character of his ancestor by our esteemed contemporary, Mr. Winthrop of Boston, in his Life and Letters of Gov. Winthrop. But the chronicles of the time display the true proportions of the man. The record of his election to be the chief officer of the enterprise does not omit to say what was thought and expected of him by his associates. It reads as follows:

"And now the Court, proceeding to the election of a new Governor, Deputy and Assistants, * * and having received extraordinary great commendations of Mr. John Winthrop, both for his integrity and sufficiency, as being one every way well fitted and accomplished for the place of Governor * * the said Mr. Winthrop was, with a general vote and full consent of this court, by erection of hands, chosen to be Governor for the ensuing year, to begin on this present day; who was pleased to accept thereof and thereupon took the oath to that place appertaining."

The civil, political and military functions, now attaching to the chief magistracy of Massachusetts, have come to overshadow all others and are the only ones now associated, in the mind, with the title of Governor. The word "Court," too, as used by us has another sense than that attaching to it in these records. When Conant, Endicott, and after them Winthrop, were selected and qualified as "Governor," the choice was made by a small body of corporators, and the electors were discharging not more a political than a commercial function. Analogies are not wanting which throw light upon this point. The title of "President," we apply in common to our highest official dignitary and to the chief officers of banking, commercial and manufacturing corporations. The word "Governor" was and is used, in England, as we use the word "President," and carries with it, of necessity, no political significance whatever. Thus the Bank of England to-day calls its executive board, as the Massachusetts adventurers did theirs, the "Governor, Deputy Governor and Company," and also holds its "Court of Directors."

I return from this digression, to quote from the files of her Majesty's Public Record Office in London, these words referring to the Winthrop emigration: "This year there went hence six ships with one thousand people in them, to the Massachusetts, having sent, two years before, between three and four hundred servants to provide houses and corn against their coming. These servants, through idleness and ill-government neglected both their building and planting of corn, so that if those six ships had not arrived, the plantation had been broke and dissolved. Now, so soon as Mr. Winthrop was landed, perceiving what misery was like to ensue through their idleness, he presently fell to work with his own hands, and thereby so encouraged the rest that there was not an idle person there to be found in the whole plantation, and whereas the Indians had said they would shortly return as fast as they came, now they admired to see in what short time they had all housed themselves, and planted corn suffi- cient for their subsistence."

"It is true," wrote the famous Capt. John Smith, in 1631, "that Master John Winthrop, their new Governor, a worthy gentleman both in estate and esteem, went so well provided (for six or seven hundred people went with him) as could be devised. But at sea, such an extraor- dinary storm encountered his fleet, continuing ten days, that of two hundred cattle which were so tossed and bruised threescore and ten died; many of their people fell sick, and in this perplexed estate, after ten weeks they arrived in New England at several times, where they found threescore of their people dead, the rest sick, nothing done, but all complaining, and all things so con- trary to their expectation, that now every monstrous humor began to show itself. Notwithstanding all this, the noble governor was no way disanimated, neither re- pents him of his enterprise for all those mistakes, but did order all things with that temperance and discretion, and so relieved those that wanted with his own provision, that there is six or seven hundred remained with him, and more than sixteen hundred English in all the country, with three or four hundred head of cattle."

Still another contemporaneous account is found in a letter of Thomas Wiggin to Sir John Cooke, Knight, principal secretary to his Majesty, and member of the most honorable privy council, dated 1632, which also gives the impression of an eye-witness: "For the plantation in the Massachusetts, the English there being about two thousand people, young and old, are generally most industrious and fit for such a work, having in three years done more in building and planting than others have done in seven times that space, and with at least ten times less expense. Besides, I have observed the planters there, by their loving, just and kind dealing with the Indians, have gotten their love and respect, and drawn them to an outward conforming to the English, so that the Indians repair to the English Governor there, and his Deputies, for justice. And for the Governor himself, I have observed him to be a discreet and sober man, giving good example to all the planters, wearing plain apparel, such as may well beseem a mean man, drinking ordinarily water, and when he is not conversant about matters of justice, putting his hand to any ordinary labor with his servants,—ruling with much mildness to the great contentment of those that are best affected, and to the terror of offenders."

Dudley, himself thirteen times chosen Deputy Governor, and four times chosen Governor over Winthrop, wrote thus from Boston in 1630, to his patroness and friend the Countess of Lincoln:

"We sent Mr. John Endicott, and some with him, to begin a plantation and to strengthen such as he should find there, which we sent thither from Dorchester and

some places adjoining. From whom the same year, re-
ceiving hopeful news, the next year, 1629, we sent divers
ships over, with about three hundred people, and some
cows, goats and horses, many of which arrived safe.
These, by their too large commendations of the country
and the commodities thereof, invited us so strongly to go
on, that Mr. Winthrop, of Suffolk, who was well known in
his own country and well approved here for his piety, liberality, wisdom and gravity, coming in to us, we came to
such resolution that in April, 1630, we set sail from old
England with four good ships, and May following eight
more followed, two having gone before in February and
March, and two more following in June and August, besides another, set out by a private merchant. These
seventeen ships arrived all safe in New England, for the
increase of the plantation here this year 1630, but made
a long, a troublesome and costly voyage. Our four ships,
which set out in April, arrived here in June and July,
where we found the colony in a sad and unexpected condition, above eighty of them being dead the winter before;
many of those alive weak and sick; all the corn and
bread amongst them all hardly sufficient to feed them a
fortnight, insomuch that the remainder of a hundred and
eighty servants we had the two years before sent over,
coming to us for victuals to sustain them, by reason that
the provisions shipped for them were taken out of the
ship they were put in, and they who were trusted to ship
them in another failed us and left them behind. Where-
upon necessity enforced us, to our extreme loss, to give
them all liberty, who had cost us about £16 or £20 a
person, furnishing and sending over."

John Winthrop, as his biographer well says, was fully
justified by these varied testimonies in saying of himself,
in a statement of his reasons for joining the New England

enterprise, "It is come to that issue as, in all probability, the welfare of the plantation depends upon my assistance. For the main pillars of it, being gentlemen of high quality and eminent parts, both for wisdom and Godliness, are determined to sit still if I desert them."

But Winthrop did not desert them and they did not sit still. Here too, on this June afternoon, was Dudley the Deputy, chosen on board the Arbella to the second place in the government, after it became certain that his predecessor, Humfrey, must take passage later. He had been associated, in a responsible charge, with the House of Clinton and Lincoln, now dukes of Newcastle, the best family of the time, Mather says, in the British Peerage : a family out of which such friends of America as Humfrey, the ill-starred Johnson and the young heir of Sir Ferdinando Gorges had chosen consorts. Thomas Dudley was now fifty-three. He had read law ; fought as a captain, both for English Queen Bess and French King Harry of Navarre ; had extricated, by his prudent administration, the estates of the young Earl of Northampton from disastrous entanglements, and was now to become the founder of Cambridge, in New England, and the first Major General of Massachusetts, and to be elected year after year, either Governor, Deputy Governor or Assistant of the Colony.

Here, too, was Saltonstall, Winthrop's first assistant, "that excellent knight" as Mather calls him, a figure not less conspicuous, from his rank, resources and character, than any other after Winthrop in the company. He was a person of sufficient consideration to have been the first-named associate of six original patentees of Massachusetts Bay. When Gov. Cradock's proposal for the transfer of the government of the colony to our soil was to be debated, *pro et contra*, before a general court, convened for

that end at Master Deputy Goffe's house in London,
Aug. 29, 1629, at 7 o'clock in the morning, Sir Richard
Saltonstall was the first-named of the committee selected
to advocate the transfer; and at a general court, held
Oct. 15, 1629, he was chairman of a committee to arrange
and draw up the terms of the transfer, to be executed
"between the adventurers here at home and the planters
that are to go over." Joining Cradock's enterprise a year
before, and now 44 years of age, he took, at once, the
leading place to which his rank, his gifts, his fortune and
his legal training entitled him; was the first signer and
promoter, if not the writer, of liberal church covenants,
and of letters of wise instruction to Governor Endicott
and the Salem clergymen, and was destined on his return
to England to sit in judgment at the trial for high treason
of five peers, in the High Court of Justice.

But Sir Richard had better claims than these to present
remembrance. He took it upon himself to rebuke the
prevailing intolerance of his time in language as courteous
as it was bold, addressed to the Boston clergy. He
writes to them as "Reverend and dear friends, whom I
unfeignedly love and respect." These are his timely
words, written from London a few years later. Fortunate
for New England had they been duly pondered!

"It doth not a little grieve my spirit, to hear what sad
things are reported daily of your tyranny and persecutions
in New England, as that you fine, whip, and imprison
men for their consciences. Truly, friends, this your
practice of compelling any in matters of worship to do
that whereof they are not fully persuaded, is to make
them sin, for so the apostle tells us, and many are made
hypocrites thereby, conforming in their outward man, for
fear of punishment. We pray for you and wish you
prosperity every way, and hoped the Lord would have

2

given you so much light and love there, as not to practise those courses in a wilderness which you went so far to prevent. These rigid ways have laid you very low in the hearts of the saints. I do assure you I have heard them pray in the public assemblies that the Lord would give you meek and humble spirits, not to strive so much for uniformity as to keep the unity of the spirit in the bond of peace. I hope you do not assume to yourselves infallibility of judgment, when the most learned of the Apostles confesseth he knew but in part and saw but darkly."

Then there was the preacher Phillips, another Cambridge man, thirty-seven years of age, the first pronounced congregationalist in the Colony—an independent theologian, standing alone among the clergy but in full sympathy with the broader views of Saltonstall and Browne—. whose resistance to a church tax in 1632 is thought to have resulted in the instituting of our legislative house of representatives. And there were the Johnsons, Isaac and his young bride, whose untimely deaths were soon to invest the Winthrop enterprise with painfully romantic interest. Besides being one of the youngest, the groom was by far the richest of the company, and the largest adventurer in the joint stock also. Not three months more remained to him on earth, and in a will made before leaving England, of which the great Hampden was named executor, he had left his estates in part to the enterprise in which he had embarked his life. When his hour came, he declared that whatever was sacrificed in the furtherance of so great a work could not be wasted, and such was the affection in which his neighbors held him, that as one after another to the number of two hundred fell asleep that fatal winter, until the habitations of the living failed to keep pace with the sepulchres of the dead, they found consolation in the fact that their kindred were resting by the grave of Johnson.

His lovely bride, flitting athwart the strong light of history for a moment, to vanish in the next, as the bright insect of a day flits across the sunbeam, gathers to herself all the poetry and sentiment of this puritanic picture. The good ship "Eagle," bought for the admiral and pilot of the fleet, had been rechristened the "Arbella" in her honor, and though her resting place may be unknown, no nameless grave can hide the memory of her virtues, while the ship "Arbella" keeps on her silent voyage down the ages. She had come, as was said in the quaint diction of the times, "from a paradise of plenty and pleasure, in the family of a noble earldom, into a wilderness of wants." All too willing to follow her young spouse wherever he might lead her on earth, she sojourned but a little here and herself led the way, anticipating him by a month, on the everlasting journey.

Small as the colony was, the little Endicott cottage, with all its early fame for unbounded hospitality, was hardly large enough for those who made haste to welcome the coming Governor and his suite. But just beyond it, on the west, lay the principal thoroughfare of the village, laid out in the beginning, as it runs to-day, four rods in width from river to river, across the narrowest portion of our narrow town. The boat landings at either end have disappeared, as the coves of North and South River have given place to solid ground. Beneath its entire length thunder incessant trains freighted with life and wealth, and shake the sods where the Governor's children played, as though riven by an earthquake. The Governor's cottage stood on this highway, not far from the corner now formed by the southeastern intersection of Federal and Washington streets. And just beyond the Governor's "fayre house," was a spot west of the street and not far from the present site of the Sewall-street Meeting House, which was at once the highest central elevation in the town, and also the common point nearest the head waters of both the North and South River. A creek from the South River crossed the street now named for Richard Norman, extending nearly or quite to the site of Mechanic Hall, while the Court Houses occupy land which bounded another cove pushing in from the north. Being the defensible point of the little peninsula, this had been chosen, perhaps by master gunner Sharpe, who lived near by, as the site for a blockhouse fort. It was known as the Arbor Lot, or, being at the head of the harbor, I am inclined to think, as the Harbor Lot Fort.

In this rude fortress doubtless reposed, for safety, the authenticated duplicate of the Charter of Charles I, as well as the silver seal of the company, the only one ever struck, both forwarded to Gov. Endicott by Higginson's fleet the year before. Here, too, hung suits of armor,—the halberds and partisans; the cuirasses of brass and corslets of chain and leather; the match-locks and snaphances, "four foot in the barrel, without rests" each with its bandoleer and bullet bag; the pikes and demi-pikes; the gorgets and helmets; the swords with cow-hide belts.

Here, too, frowned from the parapet of this strong house the five great pieces of ordnance, so scrupulously consigned by the company in London in 1629 to the care of master gunner Sharpe, and which now and again belched out their thunders to awe the feeble remnant of a wasting race. Here met, for the first meeting house was not yet built, the congregation for worship, the heads of households for government, the young for catechising, the able-bodied for the manual of arms. Here Higginson may have preached that first sermon before Winthrop, which was to prove the last sermon of his life. From these wooden battlements was to be had the most sweeping survey of the novel scene, and to this spot Master Endicott and his distinguished guests without doubt repaired, for a better acquaintance with the people and the place.

Nearly in front of the fort, stretched towards the east the narrow lane, since grown to Essex street, which connected the Arbor Lot and its cleared training field or esplanade on the eastern side, with that swampy tract extending from Shallop, now Collins Cove, and Planter's marsh, to the site of the Franklin Building. Part of this marsh became successively the Town Swamp, the Training Field, the Common, the Mall, and now Washington Square. Pleasant street, and parts of Brown and Winter streets have since been cut through it on the one side,— Forrester, once Bath street, on another. But long after Winthrop's time it extended to the line of Essex street, including the creek which as late as 1802 gave Bath street that name. And this marshy tract was almost met by a cove flowing up from the harbor on the Elm street side about as far as the church of the Immaculate Conception. Thus the narrow neck upon which Conant and his men planted themselves in 1626 to await the recruits and succor promised by the Rev. John White, of Dorchester, was nearly severed by the inroads of the sea at two several points, not far from Washington street on the west and Washington Square on the east. Between these points, on this "pleasant and fruitful neck," as Conant's friend Hubbard describes it, nestled the cottages of the early planters. The hamlet had grown, from the half score of houses which Higginson found in 1629, to a habitation for half a dozen scores of people, in 1630.

And this was the scene upon which Winthrop, Saltonstall and Dudley looked from the Arbor Lot Fort, under the mellow light of waning day. Higginson lived at the site of our Post Office, and Skelton at that of the Police Station. After these and Gov. Endicott, no persons were held in more esteem than Roger Conant, John Woodbury and Peter Palfray. It cannot be but that these worthies gathered at the fort. And Brackenbury, too, had come in his shallop from Bass River Side, and Jeffrey from Jeffrey's Creek, and Masconomo from his tented headland perhaps had sent, in birch canoes, an embassy of good will, for there was news from England, and news from England was then no every-day affair.

Conant was there, and we can feel the pride with which he points out the first house built in Salem, the work of his hands and his residence now, standing on the spot where has lately lived and died Richard Saltonstall Rogers; Conant, the Governor at Cape Ann under the patent of Lord Sheffield; Conant, who quit Plymouth in search of a more liberal system of worship; Conant, that "religious, sober and prudent gentleman," whose firmness alone, when threatened with desertion, saved to Endicott the foundations of his colony. The cottage east of Conant's is Peter Palfray's, and that west of Conant's is John Woodbury's, and Woodbury was there, for he was Conant's right hand man,—the first constable of Salem, selected in 1627 for a difficult mission to England, which he discharged with credit, and which must have made him acquainted with the promoters of the enterprise this day arriving; Woodbury, of whom since he was an ancestor of mine I may be pardoned for speaking with peculiar interest. Endicott himself was there; Endicott, oftener reëlected chief magistrate than any other Governor of Massachusetts; Endicott, of whom the exhaustive address delivered by his distinguished namesake and representative, Judge Endicott, two years ago, has left us nothing to say,—all these were there. Nor is it hard to guess the topics to which conversation leaned. The panorama before them was abundantly suggestive. Within its charmed horizon lay the bay then, as to-day, tossing and sparkling in the glancing sunlight, dotted with islands now fresh with verdure, but then dark with forests—and locked, as now, within the wooded heights of the north shore and Naugus Head. On right and left the crystal currents of our lazy streams moved on, unvexed by bridges, to the sea, and there no friendly beacon warned the adventurous boatman of hidden ledges,—at night, no hospitable lighthouse called him home. And beyond all, the ocean, changeless, yet ever new, unscarred by time !—

Such as creation's dawn beheld, thou rollest now!

Across the rivers, in North and South Fields, might be seen the outlying farms of planters, where Indian and settler plied the hoe together, while the birch canoe, and the dug-out, called their water-horse, threaded each silver stream which served them for a lane. Roads they had none. Venice in all her arrogance of wealth had not such leagues of water for her streets. Here on the south curled the wigwam fires of the Indian Camp in Forest River Valley. Here, close at hand, rose the pallisadoed fort on Castle Hill. Turning to the north might be seen the shipyard from which, the year before, Moulton and his men sent out the first craft of considerable size ever launched into the waters of Massachusetts. While across North River and fronting the Governor's house ranged themselves in straight, well ordered lanes flanked with small patches of pumpkins, tobacco and maize, the smoky huts of another Indian village,—the sagamore's town,—

oblong habitations, framed of birch saplings, covered
with mats of flagging, in weaving which, Indian girls
anticipated the æsthetic culture of household art, and
together wearing the aspect of a camp of ornamented
ambulance wagons, dismounted from their wheels. And
everywhere beyond, spreading away, until the eye grew
weary, dark, illimitable, impenetrable forest, pathless,
vast and unsubdued.

Such was the picture for whose fit setting the Topsfield
hills reared their dark frame against a northern sky. But
what added charm would the picture acquire, could we
but fathom the thought of those who looked upon it, with
Winthrop, for the first time to-day! They were no
pigmies, set by force of accident on a lofty pedestal and
growing smaller as they rose. Before embarking in this
venture they had counted its cost and grimly questioned
the future. They had not turned their backs on English
homes like theirs from any mean anxiety to better their
estates. The oppressions from which they fled would
not have weighed on minds of meaner mould. They had
not sacrificed and endured and braved,—they were not
looking to sacrifice, endure and brave, without some
consciousness of the great part they had been called to
play. The world was to profit by their losses and to be
a partner in their gains. They knew, when Conant re-
solved to stay at the hazard of his life, though all others
left him, that it was the future more than the present
which hung upon his will. They knew, when Endicott,
with that stout soul of his, struggled alone to evolve a
polity out of a state of things no prescience of statesmanship could foresee, administering law, repelling force,
conciliating the old planters, apportioning the lands, that
it was the English Commonwealth, now not far away,
which stood militant, in his person, on this virgin soil.

They knew, when Winthrop released from bonded service all the indentured labor of the company, putting his hand to ordinary work with the humblest, when not preoccupied with official duty, that caste and precedence were doomed on this continent, and that rank was not to rest on accident but on manhood from that day forth forever.

Some gleam at least of the dawning glory had reached their vision. They had looked for a city which hath foundations—a tabernacle that shall not be taken down. They were not to die without a vision of the land of promise. In this strong soil they had planted the tree which God has given us to water,—which was to spread its branches mightily,—to defy the tempest and to gather the world to its umbrageous shelter.

May we not hail it as a happy omen for Massachusetts Bay, that while our Plymouth neighbors landed in the dreary winter solstice, the longest day of our leafy summer solstice welcomed the arrival of Winthrop? But the longest day has an end. Twilight is creeping on, and the entry of this crowded experience in the Governor's journal closes at last. These are his words: "At night we returned to our ship, but some of the women stayed behind. In the meantime most of our people went on shore upon the land of Cape Ann, which lay very near us, and gathered store of fine strawberries. An Indian came aboard us and lay there all night." Here ends the record. Winthrop, with his council of assistants, had returned before nightfall to his gallant ship. Shall we leave him there, standing apart upon that lofty quarter-deck of the Arbella, his face set westward, as his heart had long been wedded to the future,—"revolving many memories,"—sighing for the morrow with its first taste of the Sabbath rest of New England,—peering into the open gates of sunset, until their purple glories faded into night,—and forecasting, it may be, the destiny of a new-born world?

God said,—I am tired of kings;
   I suffer them no more;
Up to my ear the morning brings
   The outrage of the poor.

Think ye I made this ball
   A field of havoc and war,
Where tyrants great and tyrants small
   Might harry the weak and poor?

My angel,—his name is Freedom,—
   Choose him to be your king;
He shall cut pathways east and west,
   And fend you with his wing.

I will divide my goods;
   Call in the wretch and slave:
None shall rule but the humble,
   And none but Toil shall have.

I will have never a noble,
   No lineage counted great:
Fishers and choppers and ploughmen
   Shall constitute a State.

Go, cut down trees in the forest,
   And trim the straightest boughs;
Cut down trees in the forest,
   And build me a wooden house.

Call the people together,
   The young men and the sires,
The digger in the harvest-field,
   Hireling, and him that hires.

And here in a pine state-house
   They shall choose men to rule
In every needful faculty,
   In church, and state, and school.

Lo! I uncover the land
   Which I hid of old time in the West,
As the sculptor uncovers his statue,
   When he has wrought his best.

THE LADY ARBELLA.

A POEM WRITTEN FOR THE WINTHROP FIELD MEETING,

By LUCY LARCOM.

THE LADY ARBELLA.

Read by Rev. De Witt S. Clark, of the Tabernacle Church, Salem.

The good ship Arbella is leading the fleet
Away to the westward, through rain-storm and sleet;
The white cliffs of England have dropped out of sight;
As birds from the warmth of their nest taking flight
Into wider horizons, each fluttering sail
Follows fast where the Mayflower fled on the gale
With her resolute Pilgrims, ten winters before; —
And the fire of their faith lights the sea and the shore.

There are yeomen and statesmen; the learned and rude;
One brotherhood; jealousy cannot intrude
Between heart and heart; with one purpose they go, —
To knit life to life, a new nation, and grow
In the strength of the Lord. There are maidens discreet,
And saintliest matrons; but none is so sweet
As the delicate blush-rose from Lincoln's old hall,
  he Lady Arbella, the flower of them all.

Beloved and loving, one stands at her side,
A bridegroom well matched with so lovely a bride.
Wise Winthrop is balancing care in his mind
For the colony's weal, for the wife left behind;
And godly and tolerant Phillips is there
To comfort his shipmates with blessing and prayer:
One and all, they have taken their lives in their hand,
To be scattered as seed in a wilderness land.

(29)

There is hope in their eyes, though it gleams through regret;
They go not as those who can lightly forget
The Church, their dear mother, the land of their birth,
In the glamour that flushes an unexplored earth —
A limitless continent, fringing the rim
Of the silent sea-vastness with promises dim;
And their love, reaching back from the voyage begun,
Links Old and New England forever as one.

They drift through blank midnight; they toss in the mist,
Blown hither and thither as wild winds may list.
Moons wane, ere a glimpse of the land that they seek
Breaks the chaos of billow and fog : — though the cheek
Of Arbella grows pale, with a clear, kindling eye,
She says, "It is well that we go, though we die."
And the heart of the bridegroom beats high at her side,
In response to the undismayed heart of his bride.

And still, side by side, they keep watch on the deck,
Till the faint shore approaches, — an outline — a speck
That wavers and sinks, and arises again,
Undefined, on the outermost verge of the main.
And lo! on a golden June morning, a smell
As of blossoming gardens, borne over the swell
Of the weltering brine; cliff and headland that dip
Their green robes in the sea, leaning out to the ship!

And shining above them, afar on the sky,
Where the coast-line trends inland, the snow summits high,
A glimmer of crystal! The lady's rapt gaze
Lingers long on that wonder of filmy white haze,
As a vision of mountains celestial, that rise
On the soul of the dying, who nears Paradise!
Did she know, could she dream, that to her it was given
But to touch at this new world, and pass on to heaven?

There looms Agamenticus, beckons Cape Ann;
There a smoke-wreath reveals Masconomo's red clan,
Or the camp-fire of settlers, and here a canoe —
Here a shallop steers out to the storm-beaten crew;
The low islands part, as an opening door,
And they glide in, and anchor in sight of the shore,
Where the wild roses' fragrance, the strawberries' scent
With the music of song-bird and billow are blent.

Did the Lady Arbella's light foot touch the beach?
Did the sweet-brier sway to her laugh and her speech?
Waves wash away footprints; winds sweep from the air
Glad echoes — fresh odors; — her memory is there!
And the wild rose is sweeter on Bass-River-Side
For breathing where once breathed the sweet English bride;
And the moan of the surges a pathos has caught
From her presence there, brief as the flight of a thought.

Grave Endicott welcomes his beautiful guest.
At last, in the wilderness, shall she find rest,
And dream of the cities to rise at her feet
In a nation where mercy and righteousness meet?
Dear Lady Arbella! so brave and so meek!
Too fragile a flower for this atmosphere bleak, —
When the rose shed its petals on Bass-River-Side,
The blush rose of Lincoln had faded and died.

But a soul cannot fail of its gracious intent;
We are known, and we live, through the good that we meant.
The seed will spring up, that was watered with tears;
If an angel looked on, through those first dreary years
Of the colony's childhood, and bore up its prayer,
The spirit of Lady Arbella was there;
And, to whatever Eden her footsteps have flown,
New England still claims her — forever our own!

For the lady arose to her womanhood then,
When gentry and yeomanry simply were men,
In communion of hardship. All honor be theirs
Whose names on her forehead the Commonwealth wears, —
Who planted the roots of our freedom! Nor yet
The blossoms that died in transplanting forget, —
The true-hearted women who perished beside
The Lady Arbella, the fair English bride!

ADDRESSES.

THE President briefly alluded to the three migrations from the mother-land to Salem previous to the one the 250th anniversary of which we this day commemorate. *1st*, the arrival of Roger Conant in 1626; *2d*, of John Endicott in September, 1628; *3rd*, of Francis Higginson, in the summer of 1629, who, soon after his arrival, organized the First Church.

We have with us to-day, Col. Thomas Wentworth Higginson, a lineal descendant of Francis Higginson, and also a member of Governor Long's staff. Shall we have the pleasure of hearing from him?

RESPONSE OF COL. T. W. HIGGINSON, OF CAMBRIDGE.

Mr. Chairman, and, I suppose I may say, Fellow-members of the Essex Institute:

I AM very glad to respond to any call, whether in behalf of that third migration, or of the governorship of Massachusetts which began with Endicott and Winthrop, and which is now represented by my worthy chief, Governor Long. But I should speak with diffidence after the eloquence to which we have listened, after the beautiful poem, whose grace was so charmingly divided between the reading and the rhyme. But for the fact that I have left the living Governor behind me, I should only have been able to represent a few dead Governors of a century or two ago. There is this sort of appropriateness in the present situation of affairs, that whereas, just about the time of the landing of Winthrop on this very spot, I fancy that Endicott and the people of that day thought there was one Governor too much, we at this moment think there is a Governor too little. [Laughter.]

I thought as I sat at your hospitable board partaking of your sandwiches with hearty relish (which I trust has always been characteristic of my race) that, if you were feeding me, I was,— retrospectively at least,— supplying you with a place whereon to feed. I do not know that you are aware that you are at this moment,— retrospectively, and supposing I had my rights,— trespassing on my property. I may be mistaken in the boundaries, but I fancy this is a part of the old Higginson farm. I think the last Higginson who was here used to welcome others to this spot, instead of being welcomed by others, and I wish to be equally hospitable. [Laughter.] I do not know that I inherit one of the personal features of Col. John Higginson, but I do wish he had bequeathed me his *Neck.* [Laughter.]

There is a common delusion that leads us to conceive our New England ancestry as tame and prosaic ; and to assume that there was nothing in its early records to call forth our enthusiasm. But there are no people in the world prouder of their ancestral tree than are the men and women who hear me to-day ; there is no view in the world that should bring up nobler, tenderer recollections than the little strip of blue ocean before your eyes. There are no records of migration, there are no records of the foundation of a city more eloquent, more dignified, more thoughtful, more touching, than the early annals of Salem, than the letters of Winthrop, and, I may say without assumption, than the journals Francis Higginson left behind him. The beauties of this place were never painted in more appropriate colors than they painted them. The story of that noble enterprise was never told in more simple, more direct language than they told it themselves. The sweetness of human feeling, the tenderness of personal joy and sorrow never have been written in any letters between husband and wife more exquisitely than they are written in the letters of Winthrop; although it is perfectly true that she was his third wife, and something of that sweetness may have come from prolonged and reiterated practice. [Laughter and applause.]

It is the agreeable task of the Essex Institute to combine, in the study of nature, and in its historical research, all that is most interesting in that period of our history. We smile at the dusty traditions in the unravelling of which some of your antiquarians spend their lives. We wonder at the hopefulness that expects any good shall result from these dull details. Yet it was the influence of precisely this material and this place that added another to the world's great authors through the genius of Hawthorne. In every step you take, every point you add to the knowledge of external nature or of the inner domestic life of that early period, the Essex Institute may be adding to the materials which some future Hawthorne, now growing up unknown, may yet employ. And if you could extend your investigations in Natural History far enough, and tell us what under heaven those red and yellow flowers[5] could have been that Francis Higginson found spread over these waters, acres at a time, in 1629, his descendants will be very grateful. I have not a doubt of his veracity, however, when I consider the fact that he was the first historian

---

[5] Mr. Higginson arrived near mid-summer. At this period of the year, great numbers of jelly-fishes (the *Cyanea arctica, Aurelia flavidula*, and other species) are observed on the surface of the water near the coast. Possibly specimens of these animals, some having the resemblance of flowers, may have attracted the notice of the voyager and have thus been mentioned in his Journal.

to point out the existence of lions on Cape Ann and the caution with which he did it. After enumerating a long list of animals he says, " The skins of all these animals have I seen, but the skin of the lion I have not seen." So particular was he about taking the responsibility of the Cape Ann lions upon himself!

I have sometimes thought in reading the accounts of these celebrations, that the Essex Institute had, in a manner, fulfilled his predictions about these animals. I am sure that so long as you have your present President and efficient committee of arrangements you will always secure a moderate supply of small lions for your platform. [Laughter and applause.]

INTRODUCES *Hon. G. Washington Warren*, of Boston; for many years President of The Bunker Hill Monument Association.

REMARKS OF MR. WARREN.

Mr. President, Ladies and Gentlemen: —

I feel rather diffident in attempting to address you after the very finished production to which we have listened. I am told that Dean Stanley when here, immediately after his arrival in this country, expressed astonishment at the zeal and reverence with which you commemorate these anniversaries. I am told he said "there is nothing like it in my own home."

A period of two hundred and fifty years carries us back a long way. If you divide the Christian Era into only eight parts, the period of two hundred and fifty years is a greater period than one of those parts. And then, sir, it is a great help to us to compare these milestones of time. By this comparison we find how easy it is to grasp the past. Why, Mr. President, we both remember the celebration of the two-hundredth year since these events occurred. I remember the year of my graduation, of hearing the great and classic Everett deliver the address on the two-hundredth anniversary of the arrival of Governor Winthrop in Charlestown. Perhaps you people of Salem have not yet forgiven Winthrop for leaving Salem and going southward; but if you had been living then he certainly would have remained here. We can imagine him in his boat, which was probably within sight of this place, navigating his way towards the mouth of the Mystic river, to find, as he says in his quaint language, "a place for sitting down." He arrived in Charlestown on the memorable seventeenth of June (O. S.), which seemed to typify the great event of the seventeenth of June (N. S.) that was to occur nearly a century and a half later. How significant are these dates! It is my fortune to belong to the First church in Boston, which Winthrop more than any other one instituted, and to whose covenant he was the first to put his name; and I doubt if there is anything in this country more ancient than that same covenant, which is preserved to the present day, and recognized as binding upon the worshippers.

Boston is to have its anniversary on the seventeenth of September next. Because there was an insufficiency of water, Winthrop went over the river and there had another "sitting down." And now in the Old South, on the seventeenth of September next, is to be commemorated the anniversary of this event,—the Old South which is erected on land which belonged to Winthrop. How significant! It is a great good fortune that we have preserved that historic building, not only for the connection it has with the revolution, not only for the great speeches made within its walls by the heroes and fathers of the republic, but because it marks the spot where the first governor of the commonwealth resided. And, friends, let us re-

member that it is to the exertions of the patriotic women
of Massachusetts that the preservation of this historic
landmark is due. [Applause].

I think, Mr. President, that it is a matter of congratu-
lation that the attention of our people and of the rising
generation is being more and more devoted to the colonial
history of the land rather than to the revolutionary period.
In my boyhood the principal reading-books were made up
of the language and the eloquence of the revolutionary
times ; of opposition to authority, engendering habits and
feelings uncongenial to the best growth of the intellect.
Fortunately, we can go back more than a century beyond
and dwell upon that life and those times with profit ;
back to the time when Winthrop came with christian
honor and founded this great commonwealth. And as
long as Massachusetts shall be remembered in the world
as the mother of Presidents and of Vice-Presidents, of
heroes, and martyrs, and statesmen, so long will the
memory of Winthrop be cherished as its christian founder.

INTRODUCES *Hon. George B. Loring*, of Salem, Representative in U. S. Congress from this District.

REMARKS OF MR. LORING.

Mr. President and fellow-citizens: —

I am very happy to learn from your chairman what I
represent. It seems that after dealing with the historic
governors, and calling upon the representatives of the
present race of governors, we are now to turn our attention for a short time to that valuable institution known in
this country as the General Government.

But without entering into any dissertation upon the government under which we live, I desire to call your attention to the inheritance which you can justly call your own.

The eloquent and admirable oration to which we have just listened has brought vividly before us the first steps that were taken towards the establishment of a great republic on these shores, a republic based on the fundamental principles of popular freedom and popular sovereignty. I have never been surprised at the remark of Dean Stanley that the celebration of American anniversaries greatly astonished and interested him. Well he might be astonished, for there are none like them anywhere else on the face of the globe. Can you, sir, mention a popular English anniversary? England can turn to her decisive battles, to the beheading of a king, to the futile attempt to organize a republic to end in the reëstablishment of a monarchy; but she cannot call upon her people to celebrate such events. Do you, sir, know of an event in the history of France or Germany, or Italy, or Russia, calling for a public anniversary upon which the masses of the people can gather together at the close of every hundred years, and congratulate themselves? We have a strong popular sentiment and principle which we can call our own, and which is the stamp of our nationality. Nowhere on the face of the earth is there a popular, public anniversary except upon American soil,— so far as the representative of the General Government has been able to discover.

Now, sir, that is our inheritance. I have always thought it a great thing to have an ancestry. [Laughter]. An ancestry, not a pedigree; and I have been greatly impressed to-day, while listening to the able historical disquisition of our eminent townsman, and to the beautiful word-picture drawn by a descendant of one of the founders of this commonwealth,— with the courage, the heroism of those early times, and with the wisdom and devotion which guided that ancient people in the foundation of the institutions which they have transmitted to us. Seated here on this hard barren spot of land (my friend, Col. Higginson, wishes he had inherited it; but, if he had had my experience in farming, he might think himself fortunate that the inheritance did not come to him), I have admired more and more the inheritance of this people, fastened on this barren soil. What is this rich possession? It is an inheritance unheard of before upon the face of the earth. Our fathers made us heirs of the most important movement towards self-government known in the history of the world. They gave us that marvellous decade in which, on the shores of Massachusetts, popular government was established. It is not easy to say, nor is it, perhaps, important to know, who was the first Governor of Massachusetts. It is enough for us to know that between 1620 and 1630 Roger Conant, with his little band of wayfarers, planted his feet upon these shores, and left the impress of his religious fervor; that, following him, came John Endicott, he of the mailed hand and the theological heart (is that a good expression, sir?); that after him came John Winthrop, graceful and scholarly, the grand heroic figure of these early colonial days. And shall I forget John Carver, the admirable, the honest, the pure, the godly, the self-sacrificing pilgrim? These are the four Governors who made these ten years memorable, immortal; who instituted the first popular government in the world. Roger Conant, John Endicott, John Winthrop, John Carver,—these are your ancestors. Plymouth, Trimountain, Naumkeag, Cape Ann,—these are your inheritance. What a story do they tell for the foundation of government on those principles which to-day make our republic strong among the nations of the world! You can turn to no other spot, no other decade, no other century for this glorious consummation.

These ancestors of ours who gave us these ten immortal

years came from great associations to perform without
ostentation their great deeds. They were familiar with
Milton, and had, perhaps, read with him his great protests
and his divine song. They had seen Shakespeare, and, I
doubt not, those who dared go to the theatre had heard
his inspired words spoken by his own lips. They had
admired the scientific wisdom and the political liberality
of Lord Bacon, whose star had set just before they left
their native shores. They had taken part in the great
events out of which came Cromwell and his Commonwealth. Hampden and Pym were their friends and com-
panions. No wonder they came here inspired with the
highest political purpose, filled with the sublimest religious
faith, confident and trusting—as they confided and trusted
in God,—in the power of a cultivated christian people to
govern themselves by institutions of their own creating.
And they had a vision, not of an English Commonwealth,
but of a new destiny, of an American republic, a vision
that has ripened into reality in that General Government
which I have the honor now to represent. They gave us,
in the first place, the ownership of this soil we are so
proud to call our own. They gave us the institutions
under which we live. They gave us a land-tenure pronounced by an illustrious son of an illustrious Salem
father,—the younger Nathaniel Bowditch,—to be the
most perfect system of popular conveyancing on earth.
It was not at Jamestown among that adventurous and
chivalrous band who followed the fortunes of John Smith;
it was not among the Dutch colonies at the mouth of the
Hudson; it was not among those who enjoyed the profound constitutional prerogatives laid down by the great
John Locke in the far away Carolinas,—but here on the
Higginson farm, here on the rocky shores of Plymouth
where the land was valueless, was laid the foundation

of our republic. The very barrenness of this land made us a commercial, and an inventive people, and laid the foundations of that financial prosperity which we enjoy. It was here the freedom of religious sentiment was planted and proclaimed, which gave John Endicott a perfect right to drive the Browns home because they could not agree with him, and which drove Roger Williams to seek for freedom where he did not find it. Here the suffrage of the world was established; here that decree was first proclaimed which makes it possible to take from the ranks of the people mayors of cities, representatives to state and national legislatures, delegates to national conventions who nominate successful candidates for the presidency, governors and chief magistrates in all our civil spheres and organizations,—an universal suffrage which I firmly believe will one day enable woman also to exercise her choice in the selection of those who are to make laws for the government of herself and those whom she loves. [Applause.]

These are the rights and privileges which were established here on this hard inhospitable shore, and which were proclaimed in that immortal decade,—immortal in all that makes men great and good,—great in spirit, great in toil, great in enthusiasm, great in determination, great in hope. This is the inheritance those great leaders have transmitted to us, and which we must transmit, unimpaired, to those who come after us. [Applause.]

I have endeavored to perform the duties assigned me in one branch of the general government, and I have witnessed with more and more astonishment the beneficial work born of the bitter and violent contests there. The skies may be darkened by heavy clouds, the country may seem to be threatened with sudden and sweeping disaster and ruin, but always the break has come and the blue sky shining through the rift has given us assurance that God is with us still. And when I say this I know that above all strife, above all antagonisms, above all party dissensions, above all laws and resolves of general courts, above and beyond all the disappointments that fall upon those who march along the path of political glory in this land, there is still a public conscience, there is still strong common sense, there is still an iron will. It was this "voice of the people" that gave us the victory in our great war for freedom. It was this that, when the appalling destruction of civil war burst upon us, confounding the wisdom and trying the hearts of men, brought us national redemption and increased national power. It was this that gave us the power to preserve the financial honor of the land. It was this that gave us the power to proclaim the law laid down here by the pilgrims and which has become the law of the whole people. Under the care of the good God, false counsels never have prevailed, and never will prevail in this land while this inheritance remains within us. The great doctrines of fathers are preserved to us, and to us are given in full measure the fruits of their labors. How can a government founded by them fail? How can institutions blessed by their prayers be destroyed?

As the representative of the general government, I congratulate you and myself that this work of celebrating these memorial days has fallen into hands so patient and watchful as those of the Essex Institute. I did not come to-day expecting to speak, but to listen to those words of wisdom which I always hear when the Institute meets at a Field Meeting, and your dignified and venerable leader, who believes in the greatness of our institutions, and would piously preserve the memory of those who founded them, proclaims what shall be said on such occasions. [Applause.]

44

INTRODUCES *Gen. Henry K. Oliver*, Mayor of Salem.

REMARKS OF MR. OLIVER.

MAYOR OLIVER said that after the excellent performances of the afternoon, he would not, at this late hour, trespass further upon the time of the meeting, but in a word he would express his pleasure, in behalf of the city, at this commemoration.

INTRODUCES *Seth Low, Esq.*, of New York. A son of an honored son of Salem who was educated at our schools, and now one of the most distinguished merchants in the commercial emporium of America. Mr. Low, though unexpectedly called upon, has consented to say a few words.

REMARKS OF SETH LOW, ESQ.

Mr. President, Ladies and Gentlemen: —

I appear in response to your call only as the voice of a son of Salem, who would be glad to be here but that he is on the other side of the ocean. The voice speaks, you know, in response to the promptings of the heart.

I have been told by a friend that there are no gentlemen present, except myself, under seventy years of age. Let me add that I also understand all the ladies are under twenty-five. It follows, of course, from my age, as the ladies will understand, that I have no special recollection of the landing of Winthrop, and I must lead your thoughts into some new channel.

As I stood in your Essex Institute a few hours ago, a complete set of the directories of the City of Buffalo was shown to me, and by a glance one could see the constantly increasing growth of the city. Yes, I said, this shows the growth of the city, but not its history. And so it is

with Salem. I think it must always be your pride and
glory that much of your city's history must be sought
outside of herself. Wherever your children have gone
(and where have they not gone?), there you have a right
to trace the influences, and, by consequence, the history of
Salem.

As I come here, almost a stranger, I feel as though I
was carried back to the days of your commercial prosperity. My father's career has been in commerce, as has
been mine since leaving college, and as I looked at your
warehouses I thought of the sadness that must come over
the hearts of those who knew Salem in the days of her
commercial glory, and who now look upon the changed
scene.

I do not advert to this in order to fill your minds
with sad thoughts, but with this encouraging one,—that
change does not necessarily imply decay. As I walked
through your streets almost for the first time, I was
struck by the strange intermingling of the old and the
new; and I felt that here was growing up a new life.

So long as your city has a hold on the future, as well as
on the past, there is no cause for regret. Her future will
be all the fuller because of the rich memories which
cluster about her earlier life. I congratulate you that
here in Salem, while there certainly is change, I do not
see decay. The time will come, indeed I think it has
already come, when the sons of Salem, and her sons' sons,
returning to the old city from whatever distant spot, in
the language of one of your own Massachusetts poets,
can gather here

   "from the pavement's crevice
  As a floweret of the soil,
  The nobility of labor
  The long pedigree of toil."

CORRESPONDENCE.

THE FOLLOWING EXTRACTS FROM LETTERS RECEIVED WERE READ BY REV. E. S. ATWOOD, OF SALEM.

DANVERS, 6th mo., 19, 1880.

ROBERT S. RANTOUL, ESQ.,

  My dear friend :

  I see by the call of the Essex Institute that some probability is suggested that I may furnish a poem for the occasion of its meeting at "The Willows" on the 22d. I would be glad to make the implied probability a fact, but I find it difficult to put my thoughts into metrical form, and there will be little need of it, as I understand a lady of Essex county, who adds to her modern culture and rare poetical gifts the best spirit of her Puritan ancestry, has lent the interest of her verse to the occasion.

  It was a happy thought of the Institute to select for its first meeting of the season, the day and the place of the landing of the great and good Governor, and permit me to say, as thy father's old friend, that its choice for orator, of the son of him whose genius, statesmanship and eloquence honored the place of his birth, has been equally happy. As I look over the list of the excellent worthies of the first emigrations, I find no one who, in all respects, occupies a nobler place in the early colonial history of Massachusetts than John Winthrop. Like Vane and Milton he was a gentleman as well as a Puritan, a cul-

(46)

tured and enlightened statesman as well as a God-fearing Christian. It was not under his long and wise Chief Magistracy that religious bigotry and intolerance hung and tortured their victims, and the terrible delusion of witchcraft darkened the sun at noonday over Essex. If he had not quite reached the point where, to use the words of Sir Thomas Moore, he could "hear heresies talked and yet let the heretics alone," he was in charity and forbearance far in advance of his generation.

I am sorry that I must miss an occasion of so much interest. I hope you will not lack the presence of the distinguished citizen who inherits the best qualities of his honored ancestor, and who, as a statesman, scholar, and patriot, has added new lustre to the name of Winthrop.

With sincere regard, thy friend,

JOHN G. WHITTIER.

BROOKLINE, MASS., 12th June, 1880.

My Dear Sir:

I see no prospect of my being able to be with you, except in spirit, on the 22d instant, and thus, though I united with the Institute to commemorate Endicott's landing, I must leave it to others to celebrate the advent of my own ancestor, with the company and the charter. This note requires no answer. I write mainly to renew my regrets that I am constrained to be absent from the commemoration of an event, which, wholly apart from any personal considerations, is the most noteworthy event in the early history of Massachusetts, New England, and, indeed, of our whole country. The transfer of the charter and "Chief Government" from London to New England, and the arrival of the governor and company of the

Massachusetts Bay, can hardly be counted second to any event in American annals, after America was discovered and began to be colonized.

Yours very truly,

ROBERT C. WINTHROP.

Dr. H. Wheatland,
President Essex Institute.

CAMBRIDGE, June 12, 1880.

My Dear Sir:

I am very sorry that I cannot accept your invitation for the 22d inst. That is the day of the annual meeting of the Trustees of Phillips Exeter Academy, a board of which I am President, and must therefore attend the meeting.

With hearty thanks for the courtesy and kindness of the invitation,

Very truly yours,

A. P. PEABODY.

Commonwealth of Massachusetts,

Executive Department.

BOSTON, June 14, 1880.

Dr. Henry Wheatland,
Salem, Mass. :

I thank you for your invitation for the 22d, and regret very much that I cannot attend an anniversary so interesting in itself, and which promises so much in view of the distinguished gentlemen who will take part in the exercises. I shall not be able, however, to attend as I am engaged the same day at Wellesley College. With thanks for your courtesy and best wishes for the success of the occasion,

I am yours, very truly,

JOHN D. LONG.

NEW YORK, 15 June, 1880.

My Dear Sir:

I am greatly disappointed that continued absence from home obliges me to decline your invitation to attend the Field Meeting of the Essex Institute at Salem Neck on the 22d inst.

These commemorative occasions in the history of Salem have an especial interest to me, and no one of them certainly could come nearer my heart than the 250th anniversary of the landing of those great and good men, Saltonstall and Winthrop, who left luxurious homes to help lay the foundations of this great Christian Republic.

How much I should enjoy listening to the eloquent address and melodious words of orator and poet, while sitting on the very shore where these men from the "Arbella" and their tender children first landed after their long and weary voyage!

I wish you success in your "Field meeting" and thank you for so kindly remembering me.

Very faithfully yours,

LEVERETT SALTONSTALL.

Dr. Henry Wheatland,
Pres. Essex Institute.

BOSTON, June 16, 1880.

Dear sir:

I regret extremely that my absence in the West, at the time of the meeting of the Essex Institute, will debar me from attending and listening to the proceedings of the day. I regret this the more as a like cause prevented my attendance at your Endicott Festival.

I remain very truly yours,

CHAS. LEVI WOODBURY.

Henry Wheatland, Esq.,
President Essex Institute,
Salem, Mass.

DORCHESTER, June 17, 1880.

My dear president :

Nothing would give me greater pleasure than to meet the members of the Essex Institute and to join in the services which are to commemorate the landing of Winthrop 250 years ago. But I am just off from a similar service here yesterday,— the settlement of the town of Dorchester,— being pushed into the pulpit where I was obliged to preach for a while to the people.

Not having fully recovered from the combat which I had with the pavements of the State House last year, I think it will not be prudent to go so far from home as Salem, at present, and as "discretion is the better part of valor," you will please accept this as my apology for not being with you on the 22d instant.

With profound respect,

Yours, etc.,

MARSHALL P. WILDER.

THE President mentioned that this day also commemorates the birthday of Rev. William Bentley, D. D., the pastor of the East church, Salem, and one of her most devoted antiquarians and historical scholars. It is highly appropriate to conclude these exercises with the reading, by Rev. George H. Hosmer, the present occupant of that pulpit, of the following communication entitled : —

A tribute to the memory of William Bentley, D. D., with a narrative found among his papers, of a drive by Benjamin Ward, in company with his grandfather Miles Ward, about the town, in 1760:—prepared by Stanley Waters:—

This day, which by the dutiful remembrance of their descendants commemorates the arrival upon these shores of that devoted company, Sir Richard Saltonstall, Governor John Winthrop, and other "Fathers of the New England Colony," by a happy coincidence marks also the anniversary of the birth of a man, justly entitled to rank with these honored names as a founder, though living more than a century later, of the broad and elevated civilization, in which our State and community share,—a man who joined the breadth and gentleness of Saltonstall with the efficiency and single-mindedness of Winthrop,—"the late learned and catholic Dr. Bentley," a name revered by those who sat at his feet in his lifetime, and dear to their descendants, who can, perhaps even better than they, compare his high qualities and great acquirements with those of the masters of the present time, and estimate the service his character and life have done in giving this community some of the notable qualities which have marked it.

William Bentley, born in Boston, June 22, 1759, pastor of the East church from 1783 for the rest of his life, died the evening of Dec. 29, 1819; dropping dead instantly on his return from an errand of charity that winter's night. This is not the time nor the occasion to recount his actions,— to enlarge upon his excellences. Suffice it to say that he was a man far in advance of his time, an original and deep and free thinker, yet of a truly religious nature; a scholar of a reputation not confined to his own country, and of a wide erudition; an enthusiastic student of natural history and philosophy, of social science, of languages even those of the far distant East, of statistics of which he was a careful gatherer; of history and its lessons as especially bearing upon the welfare of mankind; of politics as they affected the welfare of his native land to which he was so patriotically attached; a lover of art, a zealous antiquarian, and indefatigably industrious in collecting and recording anything relating to his studies, his pursuits, his parish, and his life.

Add to this that he was a philanthropist of the broadest views, a pastor the idol of his people, and a distinguished preacher, and we have a combination of excellences rarely to be met with in one man, and worthy of remembrance by us all.

It has fallen to me lately to inspect the rich and voluminous evidences of his talents and his industry (deposited, in the care of a society of a kindred nature to your own, but unfortunately far away from this the scene of his labors where they would be of daily service to the local student), and I send you an extract therefrom that may prove not uninteresting, considering not only the additional light thrown by it upon our early topography, and the interesting information relative to the place chosen for your meeting, but also the great affection Dr. Bentley felt for the Neck, with its beautiful scenery and interesting historical associations, as shown by its being the chosen object of his daily morning walk.

The following conversation, prefaced by a slight genealogical account, is the sole contents of a small manuscript book, found among Dr. Bentley's papers, and written by Benjamin Ward, the grandson of the venerable Miles, who was born in 1673, and died in 1764, four years after the event related, over ninety years old.

Benjamin, the grandson, was born in 1739,—a young man just of age therefore in 1760; he lived in Essex street, opposite Daniels, near the old East meeting-house, where he was a constant attendant, being also a parish officer, and a warm friend of its pastor. He died June 11, 1812. This is his account :

"My Grandfather Miles about the year 1760 called on me to get a chaise for he wanted to ride round the town. When we ware in the chaise he told me to drive down to the Neck. I asked him why the street was laid out so crooked. He answered, there was no street laid out,— that there was a swamp from Mr. Higginson's land at the corner of the common down to Collins' Cove, north of the Neck-gate ;—that when a cart whent from the Garrison on the Neck up to Town, they went by the South side of the Swamp, and when the people built, they set their houses along by the cart way, that there was a wharfe on the creek back of Mr. Gerrish's house,[c] where the shallops took in their stores, and a lane went from the Main street across Virgin Point over to Shallop Cove where they the shallops laid up in the winter season.

As we went over the Neck he told me where there was a row of cottages from the land near the Point of Rocks

---

[c] This was near the corner of Essex and East streets.

downe to the bridge to cross over to Winter Island. He
show me where Mr. Abbot's fish house stood and fish
street was that lead [ing] to Fish street wharfe, which
was about 20 rods northerly of the now Winter Island
Wharfe. That the Island was filled with flakes to dry
fish on : comeing from the Neck he shewed me where the
North Blockhouse stood, and that Pickets were set from
the blockhouse to lowater mark. I asked him where
lowater-mark was. He then said, the river above the
barr was all a saltmarsh except the channells, and one
channell came round Roache's Point and passed round
towards the blockhouse and continued round to the Creek
to the northward of the Neckgate ;—that to cross the
channell at the Picketts was up to a man's breast or neck
at lowater, after he was a man grown. I asked him
where the dirt came from to fill up the channell. He said
there was a point of land between Shallop Wharfe and
Shallop Cove to the Eastward of the lane which contained
about five acres which was washed away into Collins' Cove
and filled up the channells; that the South River was Salt
Marsh all above the point of land by Mr. Elvins' where
the flats now were except the channells and Breaks into
the Coves.

When we came up to Daniels St., he said if I would go
round by Mr. Palfray's he would show me how that river
was when he was young,— when we came near the bottom of Curtis St., he sayd, now stop the chaise, Benjamin,
and I will show you. Where the flatts now are was a
point of upland from Mr. Elvins' land[7] down so near to
Long Point as to leave a very narrow passage for the
river; the channell entered between the two points and
turned into Palfrey Cove.[8]   I asked him why that was

---

[7] This was at the foot of Daniels street.

[8] The Palfray estate was east of the Custom-house, now Palfray Court.

called Palfray Cove, he said one Palfray made fish there which he supposed gave it the name. Where the Channell came out of the Cove to Stage Point (where those rocks are was then uplands), it passed Giggles Island straight over to the North Channell,—near the turn of the channel was a brake to the Easterd that went into Palfrays Cove, where Mr. Daniels built vessels and launched them into the Cove, that there was a low swampy piece of land to the Westward of Mr. Palfray's, and a brook run into the Cove the wet part of the season. The North Channell went near strait to the Westward till it came to the burying point when it turned a little Southerly and then turned Northerly round by the piece of marsh, and so up the Millpond. The Channell between Stage Point and Giggles Island run by the now graving place into the cove, and then turned out by a long point opposite Joshua's wharf, and there come into the North Channell. The whole river above the point of land where the flats now are was salt marsh except the Channells. A brake went from the Channell into Elder Browne's Cove, another into the Cove at Ingalls' Lane, and another into the Cove at Town House Lane up to Hue Peters' Cottage, another up Ruck Creek. I then observed to him that the Point of land of Mr. Elvins' and the Marshes which had stood undoubtedly for ages should so soon disappear was to me Strange. He said it would not be so strange if you knew the then situation. The Neck and Winter Island was then a Timber forrest to the edge of the water. The first thing the white people did after they were landed was to cut the Trees off the Neck and Winter Island to dry fish on, and to fortify the Neck with two blockhouses,—that when the Neck was clear of trees, the North East wind (which before went up to Pickering Point), had a fair sweep through Cat Cove and over the low part of the Neck by

the blockhouse, up by Beckett's and Hardys, and in a
few years made a breach through the Point of land below
Elvins' Point : the cross channel soon filled up so as to
make a fair beach from Elvins land to Giggles' Island.[9]
I then asked which was the principal channel ; he said
he believed there was no difference in the depth of water,
but at Spring tides the water runs by the South Channel
to the Northward, and went up the North Channel which
made that the best, but at niptides the water did not flow
so fast and run up both channells ; both Channells were
equal except that the South was very crooked, and the
North was straight, After the breach through the point
of land by Elvins', Foot's house which was on the point
of land with some other houses that were there, were
washed down by the storms, and in a few years became
flatts, when the cross channell was filled up.
The Merchants had some difficulty in getting to the
wharf at Elder Brown's Cove, and they then contemplated
building a wharfe on Giggles' Island ; the channel arch in
the string of Union Wharfe was made where the North
Channell run ; the wharves above were built out to crowd
the channell to the southward. Major Price built his
wharf across the channell."
Here ends the quaint account of this "interview" of
1760 — would that there were many such ! — saved from
destruction by the omnivorous hand of Dr. Bentley, and
giving interesting information I am sure, to the many of
your Association, interested in Salem's early history.
Had such a Society existed in his day no more enthusiastic nor industrious member would have been found than
he, and could he have foreseen its meeting on this favorite
spot of his, — a part of that farm which he was so fond of

---

[9] Giggles Island became a part of Union Wharf.

visiting, and which had belonged to successive families of his parish, Abbot, Ives, Derby, Brown and Allen,—he would have asked no pleasanter remembrance of his birthday than this connection with it. Could he have foreseen the modern facilities of travel and improvement which have made this beautiful headland such a general and favorite resort, whose beauties had before been so little known and so sparingly enjoyed, no one would have rejoiced more than that lover of nature and of men, William Bentley.

Very truly yours,
STANLEY WATERS.

Salem, June 22, 1880.

————

NOTES.

———

A few days more of research into Dr. Bentley's "Day Book," at Worcester, have enabled me to add some extracts bearing upon the localities mentioned in the Ward "Interview," which are instructive and interesting.

In regard to "Virgin Point," and "Shallop Cove," he writes:—

"July 19, 1790. Mr. Browne delivered to me two coins, one of Lewis XIII & the other of Charles I of Great Britain. They were found upon a spot which the first settlers occupied. I intend to survey the ground, inquire the history, & search the records & then more particularly describe the coins.

21. Took a walk this morning to the spot at which the coins were found. . . . . The point after our crossing the run of water which flows from the Common to Neck Gate was called Virgin Point, said from three old maidens who lived near it the place being now to be seen. After we pass this point now in possession of Capt. Boardman & Gamaliel Hodges we come to the land upon which Vincent's Rope walk was built. There was a road into this land to Shallop Cove on the east of which was a four acre lot disposed of by the heirs of Hodges & Vincent. It now does not contain one-third of that quantity. Mr. V. & B. are now building a seawall to this lot to secure the remain-

der to be filled up level with the top of this wall. The length is ——

Beyond is Shallop Cove. It entered thirty rods beyond the present fence and is partly filled, by earth carted into it, & by means of a dyke which formerly till within a few years ran across the entrance. The sides have been plowed down, & this year for the first time the adjacent land has been plowed up by which plowing the coins were found. There was a point running out on the South side,— it had trees without the fence as it now runs in a line with the seawall in the memory of the present generation, but has entirely disappeared. Beyond is Planter's Marsh extending a considerable distance from the upland.

The first Settlers chose the North Shore by Skerry's & soon improved Shallop Cove for their fishing barks; they afterward settled Point of Rocks and made use of Cat Cove between Point of Rocks & Winter Island.

1796, Je. 29. Made an experiment at fishing from the end of Vincent's walk in Shallop Cove. It was too windy for great success.

June 1, 1803. Several buildings going on in "Pleasant Street." Old Shallop Cove is now formed into a cross street going from pleasant street to the water.

Jan. 31, 1817. Mr. Parker, son-in-law of Master Watson, has laid this week the keel of a Vessel in the old Shallop Cove below Pickman's St. This was the place of business in Salem at the first landing on this side, but the water is so shallow as to forbid much hopes of its being useful again for purposes of navigation. I suppose the whole Cove from Roache's Point to Planters' Marsh is not half the depth as when I first knew it. The conduits at the bottom of the common and along the new settlements empty into it & carry much earth."

As to the Neck and its belongings, he writes:

"Mch. 24, 1791. In conversation with Madam Renew whose family name was Abbot, I found the following facts respecting Abbot's Cove.

The inlet formed between the Island & the mainland towards the sea closed by the marsh & causeway. Her grandfather bought the house, whose cellar is now beneath the Headland of Juniper Point towards the Cove, of a Mr. Tapley. It had only a small spot of land adjoining. He afterwards bought a small house near the Causeway and owned them both. He died sixty years ago in his ninety-third year. He must have been born about 1640.

The house first purchased he kept as a public house. There is no evidence in what year the first purchase was made or that Tapley was the original owner. Abbot was, she says, of Conn., & in man's estate when he purchased. He has however given names to the Rocks, Cove, & Farm probably from the Public House he kept.

The only recollection she has of the original or former state of the

farm is, that when she was born her parents lived in the old house &
had certain privileges for taking care of the pasture as the land adjoining was then called, & that it was owned by old Col. Higginson, & by
him disposed of to Capt. Ives, & by his heirs to Capt. Richard Derby
with whose heirs it now remains. It would be a proper inquiry
whether the land came to the Col. Higginson by his father & grandfather the ministers, as that might probably ascertain the original
English Proprietors.

The informant M. Renew[10] the granddaughter is now eighty-five
years old.

Oct. 19. Colloquium habui cum Vidua Renew filia Abbot qui vixit
super the Neck terram jacentem infra Oppidum. Ipsa meminit Domum
super Insulam Winter, sic nominatam, in qua habitavit Vir nomine
Crow.

Dixit mihi de Watertown seu de ædeficiis super The point of
Rocks. Quinque domus illic fuerunt attinentia ad Waters, Harbord,
Striker, Punchard; Unius nomen non in memoriam suam venit.

Super Watch House point ædificium in quo posita est una cannon.
Duo Blockhouses prope oppidum ad introitum of the Neck. Insula
habuit plurima Fishflakes.

Abbot sold to Ives, & the whole property afterwards passed into the
same hands.

Sept. 24. . . . In the inclosure belonging to the Farm & laying
on Abbot's Cove but bounding on Winter Island near the causeway is
a mound of earth round which I traced stones set in the earth & on
each side hollows—that to the Eastward being evidently a cellar & the
other artificial, though it is smaller, & both joining in a line the mound
which is now nearly two feet above the stones. From the best con-
jectures I can at present form it was a blockhouse as I have seen the
foundations raised in this manner.

That at Fort Dummer is not unlike in a line of it though the whole
fort was an enclosed oblong without a lookout in the centre & a Blockhouse at each corner. As there was a storm of rain coming up, I
deferred digging till another opportunity. There must have been
four houses on the farm as there are the remains of the cellar & inclosure on the opposite side of the Cove.

26. This day I pursued my inquiries respecting the house of last
Saturday, and instead of a blockhouse I find by digging that this was
a very large house, & that the heap which lay so high above the
ancient method of putting foundations, is a heap of earth & stones
with old bricks & rubbish of which a large stack of chimneys was

---

[10] Matthew Renough of Marblehead was md. to Mary Abbott by Rev. Mr. Jennison,
Nov. 26, 1728.

made. Upon inquiry I find this is the old House of Abbot & not the one on the other side of the Cove, and that it was a tavern. I traced the well about forty feet north of the house, the inclosure back and the barn to the eastward of the house standing back from the road.

For my amusement I intend to pursue my inquiries & find if possible the time when last inhabited.

Ap. 11, 1795. Making inquiry into the history of the Farm upon the neck. M. Renew insists upon her particular knowledge of Tapley from whom her G. father bought the Tavern House & that one Crow lived upon the island while it was the property of Col. Higginson & that the house was deserted some time before it was taken away.

June 18, 1803. Capt. Allen building the wall towards the Cove in front of his piazza on Neck.

1807, Apr. 29. Capt. Allen has just planked his new piers on the North side of Abbot's Cove. . . . .
The waste of soil on the north side of the Neck between the bar & Hospital Point is very great annually. Acres have gone since my acquaintance with it.

Mch. 30, 1790. Found Bartlett at the new fort removing loads of wood of the old wharf upon Winter Island about a hundred yards round the point & within the wharf built by Derby. This old wharf was approached on the land over a ledge of rocks which reached to the flats & gave a security to the upper part. The old shipyard was within this wharf. Hereafter traces of this string of wharf may not be found.

June 15, 1793. Fish Street Wharf was upon the Winter Island just within the Cat Cove. The remains have been removed since my day.

May 23, 1801. Blowing of rocks upon Winter Island at the bottom of Fish Street, so that posterity will have no judgment of the form of the Shore upon which the first business was done by the primitive settlers. These rocks are for the new road which is to pass over the inlet between Fiske & Woodbridge's from Neptune St. to Water St. They have blowed also those rocks lying below the New Fort on the opposite side of Cat Cove, or Winter Island harbour.

May 16, 1790. Great preparations for launching (the Grand Turk). In digging the ship's dock four feet below the surface was found the body of a tree of red oak & sound excepting the sap. It was cut off & drawn out above twelve feet long with a crotch in the middle & two limbs.

Mar. 9, 1798. Find that there were 7 Indians found buried at the Point of Rocks at the S. W. end with those stone balls with heads supposed to be used in fishing. This land is now entirely gone.

Mr. Becket at Point of Rocks found irons & bolts which discovered a building yard on the low part towards Cat Cove.

Sawdust & chips are yet found under the mud from the Point off Daniels' Lane, Foot's formerly & afterwards Elvins' Point.

Nov. 24, 1818.   Capt. Waters informs of a large branch of a tree found at the point of flats off Foot's point which proved to be walnut. This point has disappeared since the settlement of Salem.

Jan. 21, 1819. The Oak drawn from Foot's point, see 'Essex Register' Dec. 30, 1818,—first appeared in the salt storm 23 Sept. 1815, & was thirty-five feet long & eleven inches over the butt with a crotch at the upper end.   It was in the highest possible preservation & must have been there much over a century.

I have elsewhere particularly noticed this fact.   The Clay under our land has much alum as may be seen from the efflorescence when the clay is turned out.   Allum concurs with the other salts in the preservation while buried."

"Foot's Point" lay at the bottom of Daniels' St. extending southeasterly into the South River or Harbor, and when it was washed away, the estate next north of it, owned by Richard Elvins, became the Point & gave its name to it.   Richard Elvins is called 'baker' in the deeds of his property and appears to have been a prominent man in the East Parish in his time, and to have bought real estate in other parts of it as well as this homestead.   I find no record of him after about 1744, nor of any settlement of his estate.[11]

---

[11] Two most interesting entries in Dr. Bentley's Journal, which I have since been fortunate enough to happen upon, explain the disappearance of the name of Deacon Elvins from our records, and throw clear light also upon a hitherto dark subject in the history of the East Society, the character of Mr. Jennison, and the reason of his dismission.

All knowledge upon these points had been lost as long ago as 1845, when Dr. Flint in his Farewell Discourse spoke of the entire ignorance upon the subject which existed, though it seems hardly possible that none of the elder people of the society then living were able to give some information on the matter, or that no general tradition had survived.

Dr. Flint wonders if it were some "bodily infirmity" that prevented the continuance of Jennison's labors, and Dr. Bentley more than once speaks of his predecessor's "eccentricities," but in the following explicit statement he clears away all doubt, and lifts after all these years, to our great satisfaction, that veil which Dr. Flint regretted as dropped forever.

"Mch. 22, 1801. Last Sunday for the first time since I have been in Salem, we had lay "exhortations," for the edification of the Flock.   I have not heard that this ever took place before except in a more qualified sense in our own Parish. In 1735 during Mr. Jennison's time, who was at last dismissed by consent from his known intemperance, when he was not able to attend public service, he advised Deacon Elvins to pray & read & exhort & then dismiss the assembly.

A wag once wrote on the Church door

"Our Preacher Silly Billy's sick
And we've our preaching from our Baker Dick."

Mr. Elvins was flattered by his success & instituted praying meetings at his house & finally mounted the Pulpit, & afterwards left his occupation & went & settled at Black point, now Scarborough, Maine, & married the Widow of his predecessour, Mr. Willard, & the mother of the present President of Harvard College. My Predecessour, Mr. Diman,

62

He md. July 14, 1715, Sarah Beadle, and in Dec., 1723, they were dismissed from the First Church to the East. At the former his children were baptized.

Samuel, Feb. 10, 1716-7.
Richard, Nov. 2, 1718.
Sarah, Oct. 14, 1722.
Mary, July 16, 1727.

Samuel died May 5, 1723, and the mother July 9, 1743, aged 55. I think Richard and Mary died unmarried, and that the only survivor of the family was Sarah, who md. July 18, 1744, Josiah Orne, and a Josiah Orne, jr., md. June 18, 1786, Alice, dau. of Capt. Edw. Allen, and in the person of their son—the family friend of the generation before us,—who md. his cousin Anne Allen, and removed to Pontotoc, Miss., years ago the name was revived in the familiar "Elvin Orne."

Deacon Elvins apparently lived once in St. Peters' St., as in 1743 he sold to Jos. Symonds, jr. and Jona. Verry, jr., a dwelling house and a quarter of an acre of land, bounded E. on Prison Lane, S. by the house and land of Eliz'h Gray, W. by land that belonged to Habakuk Gardner, and N. by premises of said Eliz'h Gray.

In 1728-9 he bought of Benj. Woodberry of Beverly and wife Eliz'h, and of Josiah Lee of Manchester, and wife Mary, the wives being daughters of Obed Carter, dec'd, his late dwelling house bounded

---

thought him an artful man & that he took advantage of Mr. Jennison. But in his society he was much respected till death, & his plaintive strains vouched for great sincerity in his ministry.

Sept. 4, 1799. This afternoon was buried Madam S. Orne æt. 77. She was a dau. of Richard Elvins. This Richard was a Baker in the eastern part of Salem, & Deacon in the East Meeting House. During the life of W. Jennison, the minister, he was often called to officiate as Jennison was very excentric. When he had begun he was unwilling to quit, & therefore went eastward to preach, & was ordained at Blackpoint, & married the widow of the Minister deceased, who was the mother of the present President Willard of Cambridge."

It will be seen by the following extract from a letter to the venerable society for the Propagation of the Gospel in Foreign Parts, from Rev. Mr. Brockwell, their agent then in Salem, that he characterizes Mr. Elvins a little more harshly. He is writing to the secretary at Fulham, near London, of the "New Light" doctrines then industriously propagated through this country by Mr. Whitfield and others.

SALEM, Feb. 18, 1741-2.

" Rogers of Ipswich one of this Pseudo Apostles displayed his talent in ye Town on Sunday ye 24th January & continued here so doing until ye Thursday following, when he left his auditory in charge to one Elvins a Baker who holds forth every Thursday, and tho a fellow of consummate Ignorance is nevertheless followed by great multitudes & much cried up. But I thank God, that few of my church went to hear either of them, and those yt did wholly disliked them.

" P. S. A noted teacher in this Town is suspected of Forgery, of which if he next July Court should be found guilty, I am pretty confident many of his congregation will draw off to the Church of England & more of the better sort."

N. "by the highway going down to ye Blockhouse and Neck, South by Salem Harbor. W. by land of Joseph Hillard, and E. by that of Capt. Wm. Pickering and the Collinses;" these premises — two acres in extent — " with the fruit trees, &c.," he sold to Capt. Benj. Ives Jan. 14, 1733.

This property at the head of the Neck was known as "The Block House Field."

He was one of the co-owners with Benjamin Ives and Philip Saunders in the land, dwelling-house and Windmill which were where Northey St. now runs, and in 1742 sold his quarter to Rev. James Diman.

April 10, 1721, he bought of the Rev. Benjamin Prescott and wife Elizabeth for £190, three quarters of an acre, bounded N. W. by ye premises of ye Widow Dourie, N. E. by those of Widow Sarah Williams, S. E. by the house and land of Samuel Foot, and S. W. by the land of the Higginsons, with the dwelling-house, bakehouse warehouse, fruit trees, &c., excepting its common right.

These premises were those from which the name was given of "Elvins' Point."

They had been occupied by John Stratton at a very early period, and afterwards belonged to Henry True, whose widow Israel (sic) then of Salisbury, conveyed them,—a dwelling house, quarter of an acre of land adjoining, &c.,—to George Gardner, merchant in 1659. Mr. Fitz. Waters obliges me with the conveyances from these early owners to their later successors. George Gardner died in 1679, leaving by his will the estate in two parts,—one, the southern or water end, to his dau. the wife of Habakkuk Turner; the other or northern end to his son Samuel.

The former was sold by Robert Turner of Weathersfield, Conn., joined by his sister Mary and their mother Mary Marston, in 1698, to Samuel Foot, and while in the holding of the latter was so largely washed away by the wind-driven waters, as stated by the elder Ward.

In 1702 Capt. Samuel Gardner conveys to his son and dau., John and Hannah Higginson, the house " Cozen John Buttolph lives in," with the Bakehouse. &c., &c.

Elizabeth Higginson a dau. md. Rev. Benj. Prescott, and from them, as we have seen, the estate came to Richard Elvins. In 1744 Elvins conveyed it to his son-in-law Josiah Orne. Witnesses, Walter Palfray.

Francis Cabot.

In 1748 Orne sells to John Carrell. Witnesses, Thos. Lechmere.

James Perrott.

In 1756 he recovers the same from Carrell by execution.

In 1757 he sold it to Capt. John Webb (who md. Judith Phelps, whose sister Rachel md. Daniel Hathorne), and Webb sold in 1798 to his son-in-law James Carroll the northerly portion, having earlier in that year sold the southerly part to Joseph Fogg, who I think bought afterwards the other part also and from whom the flats at the bottom of Daniels' St. took the name which they have borne in our own time, of "Fogg's Beach."

In regard to the changes of our shore, Dr. Bentley remarks about 1818, that Collins Cove was then only half as deep as when he came to Salem (1783) so much deposit having been carried into it, especially by the little creek flowing down what was afterwards East Street.

Might not Virgin Point have taken its name from John Virgin, an early merchant of Salem?

STANLEY WATERS.